I0760809

The Ruminist

Other Books by Glenn Alan Cheney

Thanksgiving: The Pilgrims' First Year in America

Quilombo dos Palmares:
Brazil's Lost Nation of Fugitive Slaves

Journey to Chernobyl: Encounters in a Radioactive Zone

Journey on the Estrada Real:
Encounters in the Mountains of Brazil

His Hands on Earth: Courage, Compassion, Charism, and
the Missionary Sisters of the Sacred Heart of Jesus

Law of the Jungle:
Environmental Anarchy and the Tenharim People of Amazonia

Promised Land: A Nun's Struggle against Landlessness,
Lawlessness, Slavery, Poverty, Corruption, Injustice, and
Environmental Devastation in Amazonia

Frankenstein on the Cusp of Something

Just a Bunch of Facts

Poems Askance

Notions from a Time of Peril

Acts of Ineffable Love

Love and Death in the Kingdom of Swaziland

How a Nation Grieves: Press Accounts of the Death of Lincoln,
the Hunt for Booth, and America in Mourning

Acts of Ineffable Love

The Ruminist

Glenn Alan Cheney

New London Librarium

The Ruminist, by Glenn Alan Cheney
Illustrations by Glenn Alan Cheney
Cover art by Gabriela Aisenberg

Published by
New London Librarium
Hanover, CT 06350
NLLibrarium.com

ISBNs
Paperback: 978-1-947074-80-4
Hardcover: 978-1-947074-81-1
eBook: 978-1-947074-82-8

Who looks outside, dreams;
who looks inside, awakes.

Carl Jung

The Ruminist

The Ruminist wishes she knew five people:

Who she thinks she is.

Who others think she is.

Who she is.

Who she was.

Who she will be.

Who she would be if.

The Ruminist perches
on a big, round rock
perched in a shallow river.

The water flows around her
so fast, it seems
she and her rock
are struggling upstream.

She clings to the rock,
not to the water.
She sees the flow as
beauty, money,
status, strength,
beliefs, and possessions,
all doomed to disappointment.

She liberates the water
as if freeing herself
from enslavement.

The Ruminist lies on a bed of moss
at the edge of a grove of poplar and ash.

It's as comfortable as can be,
soft and cool and smelling so slightly
of humid earth.

She probes her wounds.
They are well in the past now,
healed but still hurting.

She can appreciate them from the distance
her bed of moss allows.

She thinks how everyone has scars,
some seen, most not.

The first is the trauma of leaving the warm womb
for cold of the world.

Later, the loss of the breast
and the cradle of her mother's arms.

Then the insults of peers.
The scraped knee, the bumped noggin, the broken bone.

Then her first failure.
And then the rest.

She is crosshatched with scars and scabs,
tender spots and calluses,
just like everyone else.

But she's alone
on her bed of moss.

Lying on her back in deep summer grass,
the Ruminist closes her eyes to bright
sunlight.

She sees blue inside her eyelids.
"The stronger the enemy seems," she
whispers,
"the more likely its evil
is a natural proclivity.

It is a mistake to fight evil with its own
strength.
Goodness may be the best defense and
antidote,
and it may be your strength,
but if it simply will not work,
do not resort to the enemy's evil.

Devise your own."

The Ruminist is wealthy.
She can afford anything she wants.
She already has little
and wants less.

In this, she is wealthier than
the pecuniarily endowed
who have too much
and always want more.

still, she needs to work.
Her work is to find work
that isn't work.

The Ruminist doesn't have to carry a burden far
to understand that the lighter burden
is easier to carry and to carry well.

The lighter the burden,
the easier to remain calm and at peace
and the easier to carry on.

She has learned to avoid
taking on burden
to pursue less burden.

No burden is more valuable
than peace and calm.

And pursuing more
only pushes peace and calm away.

A long time ago, a friend with blue eyes
and a creaky voice intimated,
"What is stopping you from loving?

"Look for that and try to understand it.
Then love is yours."

But the Ruminist still does not understand.
She thinks she feels it,
but she does not understand.

In the claws of a relentless rain,
the Ruminist listens to the drips and drops
on her hat and shoulders.

She hears patterns
in the wet-leaf patter
all around her.

She looks at the interlocking rings
bursting outward in a puddle.

The rain seems to rain
with purpose and intent,
falling so far to make something happen.

Purpose is a compass, she thinks.
A path.
A place and reason to stand.

Cheney

The Ruminist touches her nose
to the soft petals of a rose
as her thumb presses against a thorn.

Love, the rose tells her,
is all blossoms and thorns,
male fantasies of hope,
female fantasies of escape.

The rose says to be
open like a blossom
but closed like a thorn.

Chanes

The Ruminist sits at a table
with a cup of tea, a pen,
a vial of ultramarine ink,
a rectangle of pale paper
not much bigger than her hand,

And a letter from a sad friend.

The Ruminist writes:
“Much of what upsets you
upsets you only because
it upsets you.

If you don’t let it upset you,
it ceases to upset.
Let it cease.”

In two hands the Ruminist
cups an injured nuthatch.
It squeaks three times
with pain and fear.

The Ruminist thinks,
The present lasts forever
even as it ceases to exist
at every moment.

One should take action, internal or external,
to either preserve the present
or push it into the past.

Both are continuously possible;
only one is advisable.

She I knows what should be done
but not how to get it done.
But she knows it can be done.

She holds the nuthatch
until it seems to feel better.
Then she lofts it upward.
It flies as if just learning.

The Ruminist looks into
an old, splotchy mirror
and feels like maybe
she's an example of something.

She doesn't know
whether to hope so
or to hope not.

So she keeps looking.

Wind sends a slender slip of paper
hopping to the Ruminist's feet.

Minuscule faint-blue print says,
"You are dying.
Do what the dying would do
with their last few days.

But be careful.
You may not die
for many years."

The Ruminist lays her palm
on the head of a small child
and does not say,

"Death will stop you
from doing what you do.
Will death be your friend or foil?

It depends on what you are doing.

Do something
that makes death
your enemy."

The Ruminist writes
to a confused person
in a position of power.

She says, "All souls have a counterpart,
an opposite, a nemesis.

One is good but never good enough,
the other bad but capable of worse.

Know your souls.
Nurture the one that could be better
and try to bury the other
in darkness and dirt."

The Ruminist sends a card of congratulation.
She writes:

All that is within you can be discarded.
Look hard for the parts
that should be extinguished
with your will.

You have will.
This is most of what it's for.

"Everyone has will,"
the Ruminist ventures,
"but certain demons
will always try
to corrode and corrupt it.

The struggle between them is constant.
The will must win.

If it loses–
to greed,
to anger,
to sloth,
to false and ephemeral comfort–

it withers the soul.

The person of weak will
and withered soul
is proportionately less human."

The Ruminist prepares soup.
She cuts and chops,
peels and stirs,
tastes and rolls her eyes
upward to the left.

She smells her fingers.

Actions are the bricks of the self," she thinks.
"Good intentions may be the mortar,
but it's the bricks that build
a person's inner edifice.

And just as bricks can be
an obstructive wall,
they can be pavement
for the path forward.

The Ruminist sits in the shade
of a tall, dense tree
in an open field
to think.

Thoughts vie for her attention
like a horde of toddlers tugging,
clambering, beseeching,
wanting, needing.

She chooses one thought to think:
that thinking one thought
leaves a horde of others unattended.

Alone on a trail
through oak and maple,
a path of old, wet leaves,
the Ruminist whispers,

"There is deep satisfaction
in choosing to do
what is right
and avoid what is wrong.

Choosing the temptation
of the wrong may yield
a passing satisfaction,

but it does not last,
and it eventually disintegrates
into dissatisfaction."

The Ruminist sits alone
among several people.

They jabber deeply
of the shallow.

She wants to say,
but will definitely not say,

“If you pause before speaking
to consider whether your words are true,
you will speak less.

The longer you pause and consider,
the harder it is to recognize truth.

You may end up saying or writing nothing.
Your silence may be taken for wisdom,
which,
in a silent sense,
it is.”

On a park bench,
early morning,
dressed to please others,
on her way to somewhere but stopped,

the Ruminist realizes that
opinion is rarely necessary,
and rarely does its voicing
result in anything at all.

Those who disagree
will disagree all the more,
and those who agree
will find you boring.

Weeping with a shade of guilt,
hand over wet eyes,
the Ruminist once again
tells herself
that if any human can do it,
any human can do it.

The true difficulty
is in choosing to do it.

The more difficult
the the task or talent,
the more time it takes to learn.

One cannot be a maestro musician,
a fearsome warrior, a scientist,
an athlete and a tyrant.

One needs to choose
and then to do.

Across the table from an angry man,
the Ruminist wrestles with the thought
that there is no way to tell an angry man
that anger eats the angry from within.

Anger is a weakness and a vulnerability,
and it accomplishes nothing.

Compassion and reason
are better means of reaching
the goals of anger.

The Ruminist passes a green and orange leaf
to an old friend and explains
that everything has changed and will change.

The wise look for why:
what caused the change
and to what end.

The Ruminist shudders her cloak
up over her shoulders,
settles it into place,
presses her lips together
and wraps her hand
around a door latch.

Outside: frozen rain.

Some friends are destructive,
she thinks before opening the door.
You owe them nothing,
not even a reason
for freeing yourself from them.

The Ruminist lies in bed at dawn.
She feels heavy,
tormented,
indolent,
under a crush of forces,
painful though not present:

Friends, memories, gravity,
inertia, habits, fears,
desires and obligations.

Mastery of the self-force, she thinks,
is the first step toward
overcoming the others.

But all she does is think it.

Curled up
around a secret agony,
the Ruminist tells herself,
"The harm I've suffered
is a lesson I've learned.
I am throbbing with education.
I will not wallow in pain."

Staid for a moment,
standing in her shoes,
the Ruminist remembers,
again,
that there is a time to wander
and a time to wait,
a time to stand,
a time to follow a path,
a time to wander off the path,
to wander toward
another place to wait.
At any given moment,
those are the choices.

A simple cat tells the Ruminist
to learn to use
what she cannot control,
that fate is often a hidden gift,
a message,
a lesson,
a clue,
a reminder,
a comma in an unfinished sentence.

In a chilly dew at some point
after a new moon midnight,
stars tell the Ruminist:

"The universe is infinite.
All points are at the center of it.
You are the center of the universe.
So is everyone else."

The Ruminist's predilect dictionary says,
Velleity is a wish too weak to lead to action.

But it does not say
Some velleities should be de-wished,
others fed to a point of impetuosity.

The decision depends less on the wish
than on the wished."

Cheney
'22

The Ruminist sees a certain someone
and does not say:

People are born with wings.
In childhood those wings
may be broken or left to wither,
a gangrenous wasting away.

These people crawl through life,
and who can blame those who,
in resolute hopelessness,
live as low as snakes and dung beetles?

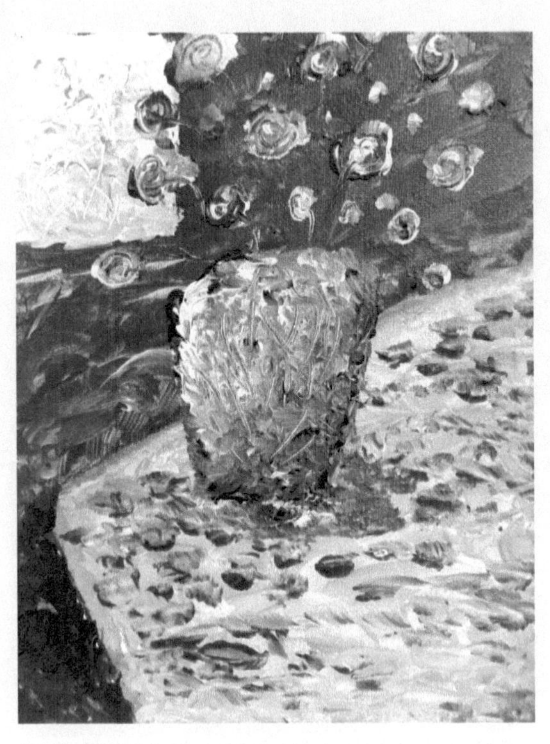

The Ruminist smashes her left thumb
with the blunt end of her grandfather's hatchet,
sticks the thumb in her mouth,
tastes rust, blood,
and a certain memory,
pulls it out when it's ready,
looks deeply into
the labyrinth of her fingerprint,
decides that all lives contain
myths at their core,
and the core of myth is message.
The message informs the myth.
The well examined life
exposes the personal myth,
and therein lies each life's
most essential message.

The butterfly must struggle
its way out of its cocoon
or it will not have the strength to fly,
the Ruminist thinks as she struggles
her way out of a certain cocoon.
She is in this way a butterfly, and
struggle is the seed of her strength.

It’s the pebble that gets her,
a stone not much bigger than an apple seed,
sitting in smooth dust the moment
the dawn sun hits it,
casting a long shadow
across shadowed grains of sand.

To see, one must look.
One must pause the passing glance
to focus inward, inward, inward
into something small, simple, and beautiful.
The veins of a dead leaf.
The dew drop on the spider web.
The swirl, dip and soar of a flock of birds.
The form of nested fingers.
The dawn shadow of that minuscule rock.
Look, then see,
then look at what you see,
then look behind it.

Crunched up in a kind of prayer
in a place dim as dusk,
knuckles enlaced and locked,
resting on her knees,
the Ruminist moves only her lips
to say with silence:

The well crafted whisper
is louder than the ill thought holler.

Truth is a feather on a zephyr.
Confidence and correctness need not shout.

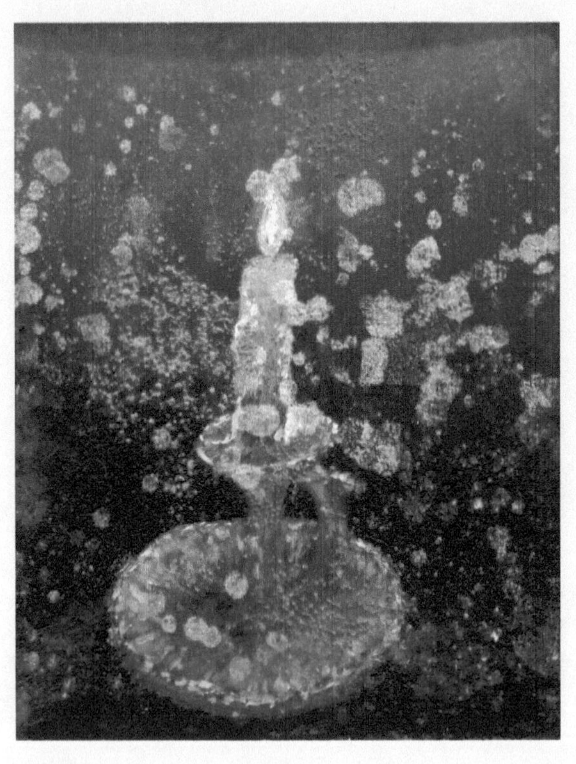

With two hands on a certain place
just above her heart,
under a raw, too-gray sky,
the Ruminist nods to accept
that sadness of soul
is a sign of vacancy,
even vacuity,
a vacuum that begs filling.

First she must fill it with calmness.
Then enlighten the calmness with imagination,
then let imagination coalesce into thought,
then thought into plan,
plan into action,
action into satisfaction,
satisfaction into joy.

That joy is all
she will let anyone see.

The Ruminist fingers flowers
into a canvas of sand.

She finds what she was looking for.
Under the flowers,
at the edge of an incoming tide,
she writes:

Words are not a message.
They are a sign pointing toward a message.

Even lies point toward truth,
just not straight toward it.

The Ruminist lies down in new snow,
stretches her legs and arms,
sweeps up and down as if swimming
until she lies in the embrace of a cold angel.

She thinks what Jesus thought,
that goodwill is the path to heaven on earth–
goodwill in community,
in business,
even in war.

Jesus called it love,
but mere goodwill would suffice.

A gesture to the other,
an attempt to understand,
an offer to relieve
the agony of anger.

It's all so easy.

The Ruminist hears someone singing far away.
The distance eats the words,
even the tune,

but something reaches her
and reminds her
that everything that has ever happened
has died.

Your vision of the past is an illusion,
the Ruminist tells herself,
not for the first time.

The past is gone, of course,
but the illusion remains.

As with all illusions,
the illusion of the past
is colored with emotion
and resistant to reason.

So be it.
But so know it.
And knowing it
will cast new color into the illusion.

The Ruminist touches one finger
to the sunny tuffet of a dandelion,
taps it to see it dip to one side,
then swing back.

She pinches it
near the bottom of the stem,
just a little.

The stem is tender, fragile, almost liquid.

Every decision, she thinks,
is a moral choice.

The Ruminist chews
on a thin stem of grass
with a fuzzy green seed-laden
tuft at the end.
She watches it dance in the air
before her face.

Reason and love,
she realizes,
are two approaches to life.
Both should be applied in all situations,
but never to each other.

The Ruminist picks up shards and chunks
of busted pottery, nesting
little pieces into big pieces.
When each piece touches a piece,
it utters a dry, raspy tunk.

She decides a broken heart
isn't really broken
unless it never gets to get broken again.

The Ruminist looks deeply into her reflection
in a dark pool of water
under a dome of autumn leaves.
Can you ever understand your own soul? she asks it.
Its shimmer seems–seems!–to say:
"Only if you listen to it,
and only if you know it's your soul
and not something else."

A person's wealth
is of no account,
the Ruminist thinks at a man
with his nose too high
in his own golden glow.
What counts is how it was gained,
how spent.

The Ruminist seeks and savors
bewilderment.
It's more enlightening than certainty.
Certainty is always a matter
of organized blindness.
Bewilderment
is eyes wide open.

Worry, guilt, and love
are fuels for action,
not ends in themselves,
she reminds herself
under duress
in the middle of the night.
Put them to work,
she tells herself,
or put them aside.

The Ruminist leaves
autumn leaves where they lie.
She likes the warmth of the oranges
as they toast in the cold.
She likes the sound
of scuffing through them.
She likes to watch them in the wind,
running,
leaping,
pirouetting,
forth and back, yon and hither,
free and wildly decisive like children
playing in a field
until snow howls in
and they all blow away.

Slow, silent, fat flakes of snow
twirl around the Ruminist,
each to settle into its own spot.
It is best not to push
that which is flowing
in the right direction, she figures.
And it would be foolish
to try to make it find a better course.
The ease of the flow leaves time for
appreciation, gratitude, and correct action.

The Ruminist sprawls
in dappled light
under an apple tree.

It seems a perfect place to be.
Anywhere else would be worse.

Sore in flesh and mind,
she wanders in her own stasis.

She mulls the fuzzy little apples above her.
They seem to know what they're doing,
how they got there, where bound.

She has nothing but questions.

Does purpose require plan?
Does plan require purpose?
Is purpose a burden or liberation?
Can purpose be found along the was?
Should one wait for purpose
or wander off looking for it?

And is wandering
a kind of waiting?

The Ruminist sits in a quiet corner
in a vast room of people standing.

She is content alone,
knowing that words are weight.

Silence is the lightest burden.
Silence leaves conflict
in a weightless void.

Silence says what words cannot.
It is space when space is needed,
which is always.

The Ruminist plucks a stamen
from a blossom of honeysuckle,
touches the infinitesimal
drop of nectar to her tongue.

The tiny drop reiterates
that the person with five houses is poor
because the wealth leaves no time
to enjoy them.

Possessions consume time
and become a burden.

Status by possessions is foolish.
Status should be measured by
how much time a person has,
and wealthy is the person
free of burden
with time to do nothing.

The Ruminist finds an old quarry
in the woods, a narrow canyon
cut into a hill long ago.

It seems not to belong,
the tall walls of stone
moist with rock sap
flourished with fern,
coated with moss,
dim with distant light.

In such a strange place
she finds a strange place,
a dim canyon in her mind.

Can we save our mind with madness,
she wonders; she wonders:
Can we take madness
as a privilege and responsibility?

It's a long, dark walk
through blustery sleet
one night for the Ruminist.

Her feet and ankles
are wet and sorely chilled.
Slush goos from her hat.

Then she wonders
whether purpose needs adversity,
then whether she needs adversity
to find purpose.

In music,
the Ruminist thinks,
lies proof of soul.

Music reaches inside people
to a place science and facticity
could only dream of going
if they could dream.

The nature of children,
experienced by everyone,
is as mysterious as music.

What music and children do
in the deep, unseen place
cannot be measured,
depicted or described.

Yet everyone is sure
that there is such a place.

In a dusky place,
the Ruminist skips a flat rock
across the mirror of a crepuscular pond.

Each spot the rock kisses
sends ripples outward.
Seven spots before the stone sinks.

The seven circular ripples
overlap and jounce each other.
The outward ripplings
soon ripple into each other.

Reflections wobble.
From her dusky place
the Ruminist figures
the duty of all adults
is to turn their suffering
into the joy of children.

Each child is a spot
kissed by a skipped rock
sending ripples outward into others.

If I never err,
the Ruminist thinks,
I haven't reached far enough.

She thinks this deep
in a puddle of shallow goof.

Every error should be
an element of education.

The unerring are fools
who care more about safety
than education.

There is little education in safety.
The Ruminist likes her puddle of goof.

The Ruminist lies naked
in late June sunlight and tall grass.

The sun and grass on her bare skin
say success is a negative accomplishment:
a life freed from desires
for possessions, status, attention,
money, pride, greed, and gluttony.

If success is to be a positive accomplishment,
let it be the attainment of
inner peace,
outer calm,
the presence of love,
the confidence to exercise kindness.

How long must one
lie in June sunlight
to declare victory?

The Ruminist delves
into her moonlight shadow.
Within us, or behind us,
she thinks,
is the shadow of ourselves,
the part of us unenlightened
(but very close, enshadowed),
touching us at the heels,
following us,
but always sheathed in darkness.

In a cavernous church
the Ruminist stands
before the image of a saint.

The icon depicts the kind of suffering
a person feels when punctured by arrows,
fully aware that he deserves it.

In a kind of prayer
the Ruminist intimates
that change in character
does not reflect
a lack of integrity.

It reflects experience.
The change is a step toward wisdom
born of arrows and away from the sweet,
simple wisdom of childhood.

Sitting on a stump in a forest of snow,
the Ruminist thinks back on a heartthrob.

Back then, her heart throbbed
whenever it could.

Love was a whirlwind
of dizziness, purity and heat.

It turned her into
something like a child.

But childhood has a way
of growing into something else.

Cheney
'22

The Ruminist holds a cold frog,
sack of amphibial ooze,
in such a way that its head peeks out
between her thumbs.

She can feel it breathing.
It does not blink.
Close enough to kiss it,
she whispers:

There's wisdom
in every nook
of being trapped.

Then she opens the trap,
and the illuminated frog
flies into the air.

On a leaf of paper
the Ruminist writes:
You are the product
of all that has happened to you.

All that has happened to you
constitutes that trauma of yourself.

You are what
your trauma has made you.

Being born
was just the beginning.

Now is the unending end.

She folds the paper
into a neat triangular package.

Later, she will set it
on someone else's path.

The Ruminist holds sand in a fist.
The sand trickles out
like time through an hourglass.

It means nothing, but she can feel it,
and feelings, she thinks,
can grasp what meaning can't.

Sometimes the Ruminist has to tell herself
to look for a direction.
To look for a path.
To look for intention.
To aim with purpose.

She tells herself to walk
slowly in one direction,
one foot on the earth,
the other above the shadow of itself
at the lowest level of sky.
And to keep going.

One thing the Ruminist knows for sure:
There is no point of satiation
for spiritual striving by physical means.

Each desperate gulp of stuff
pushes satisfaction farther away.

The Ruminist sits on a tuffet
in the shade of a tulip tree.
Down comes a spider,
hanging by an invisible thread,
a web of a single strand.

She is not frightened.
She offers it a dollop of curds,
a smidgee of whey.

The bug swings in an infinitesimal breeze.
It says nothing, and neither does she.
Neither of them needs to.

The Ruminist stops walking
in a place so dark
she can see nothing

except what she's thinking.
The entire content of her mind,
she's thinking, is illusion.

Her illusions are a swirling assortment of
the entertaining,
the lethal,
the overwhelming,
the distracting,
the instructive,
the urgent and the disregardable.

And she sees that there are two of herself:
one only in her mind,
suffering the continuous barrage of illusions,
the other the physical Ruminist
suffering the continuous onslaught
of the physical world.

The Ruminist watches a maple tree
in autumn as the dawn light
touches the top and bit by bit descends.

The orange leaves detach
as the light hits them.

She is entertained,
fascinated,
thrilled to watch
the inevitable and uncontrollable unfold
so gently, so quietly.

She wonders if all things
inevitable and uncontrollable
would have it any other way.

The Ruminist rests
on a bench a public space.
She hears someone say,
"I told myself not to do it."

She has heard herself say that, too.
She asks herself:
Who is the you who tells you what to do?
Why can't those two get along?
Or become one?

Sitting on a vast flat rock
halfway up a mountain,
a dog's chin in her lap,
the Ruminist senses that the dog
is showing her that emotion
may be fog to reason
but it's clarity into places
reason cannot go.

Burdened
as if within layers
of hot, soaking-wet wool,
the Ruminist comes to suspect
that attachment to a thing is one thing.
Attachment to illusion is the same thing.

The Ruminist doesn't just blow her nose.
She blows it with the realization
that letting go of something,
be it a possession or a thought,
is always an act of liberation.

Deep within the dark of warm blankets
the Ruminist whispers to herself
and to her other self,
that it's absurd to be a prisoner
of her own thoughts
or her other's thoughts,
that thoughts should be tools,
not weapons of the other,
not jailers of the self.

The Ruminist keeps thinking.
Thought, she thinks,
can prevent action
by drowning the mind in possibilities.

Few of those possibilities
are probable or desirable.
Many are merely fears of inactionability.

They can be disposed of readily,
clearing the mind for the thought
more likely to lead to action.

The Ruminist scuffs through ankle-deep leaves,
crackly dry leaves of maple, black birch and oak.

The pace of the rustle
says one's own life is infinite.
It's all there is,
the totality of everything,
for if it ends,
everything disappears.

And one's own life is infinitesimally short
in the infinitude of eternity.
One must be swift to love
and make haste to be kind,
for affection loosens the greedy,
mollifies the evil
with the harmless hush
of crackly dry leaves.

The Ruminist looks at plain white paper
for a long, long time, wondering
what's within blank space.

Is mystery a lie, she wonders,
or a space to lie
or a space available for a lie,
or a truth we can't quite see?

The Ruminist reads,
but then she has to stop
to think:

How much of our pleasure
is a pool of illusion and blindness?

The Ruminist trudges
through a tundra of confusion.

If it were easy,
she tells herself,
I'd never get there.

An acorn plops
into an eddy in a creek.
It floats around and around,
bobbing just a bit
in the indecisive gyration.

A yellow leaf slides
down the dark water,
around the rock
and into the eddy.

The leaf and the acorn
kiss and linger
as they waltz
within the circle.

The circle widens
until leaf and seed
drift out and then
down the tea-dark stream.

The Ruminist can't decide
whether she's in a parable, a fable,
an apologue, an endless saga,
or a sad and beautiful myth.

The Ruminist holds a calico rabbit
in a nest between her breasts and thighs.
The rabbit wiggles and squirms,
wiggles and squirms,
then stops.

All it does then is breathe.

The Ruminist doesn't know
whether love is constant,
if truly true,
or whether it is always
either rising toward
the peak of all a person can feel
and then necessarily, inevitably,
begins to deteriorate.

The Ruminist lies alone in the dark.
She is warm under blankets.

The warm, creamy light
of a full moon
slips under her window shade.

She hears nothing but her own breath.
She wonders whether love
always stands at the abyss of loneliness,
whether that also applies to grief.

If it feels like love but isn't,
is that good enough,
she wonders on a granitic boulder
odd on a grassy hill.

It's a gritty, grainy boulder.
Its flecks of feldspar
poke into the skin of her scapula.

If it doesn't feel like love but is,
is that so bad?

Her fingers slide rough circles on the rock.
It's a good rock, and she's glad to touch it.

The Ruminist paints a picture with her fingers,
a dab of color on each of eight.

The picture looks like maybe
it's a field of flowers
or a full-color cave drawing,
maybe a throng of orphans
or the unseen side of a distant planet.

Incomprehension can be a good thing,
she figures, a privilege
but also a responsibility.

She will wash her fingers, but not yet.

Within the draping embrace
of a tall, broad weeping willow,
the Ruminist hugs hers head
and weeps gently
into the lap of one arm.

Cruelty feeds off the vulnerable,
she knows and has long known,
and she knows she was and still is vulnerable.

Everyone else is, too,
even the cruel.
Loving, she reminds herself,
is an act of courage.

Hands of fern
and fingers of fiddlehead
nest the recumbent Ruminist.
Oak overarch.
Shaggy vines wend up through the green.

From her recumbent perspective,
everything that grows
points in the same direction.

Alone on a trail among December trees,
a path of old, wet leaves,
the Ruminist whispers
someone who isn't there:

There's deep satisfaction
in choosing to do what is right
and avoid what's wrong.
Choosing the temptation of the wrong
may yield a passing satisfaction,
but it does not last,
and it eventually disintegrates
into its opposite.

The Ruminist talks with a knotty old man
from a foreign country, Rumania, maybe.
He speaks no French nor she Rumanian,
but he is clearly asking for work.
He extends his gnarled-leather hands
as proof of honesty and effort,
his curriculum vitae written in fissures.

She asks him to dig
The deepest, widest hole he can by sundown.
He doesn't understand, or can't believe,
what she's saying,
but when she hands him a shovel
and points to the ground,
he knows what to do.

She brings him water, cookies,
a plate of hot food,
all the carrots he can eat
and a fistful of money.

She doesn't know what the hole is for.
Maybe she'll plant something.
Maybe she'll bury something.
Maybe she'll just leave it there,
a hole for another day.

Cheney

The Ruminist tucks tight
within blankets
hours before dawn.

She pulls the blanket over her head
so she can inhale herself.

A voice within her says
imagination can give you deep pleasure
and terrible suffering
though it's entirely illusion.

Can we say that imagination exists
but its pleasures and pains do not?

Can we control our imagination
to turn the illusion of pain
into the illusion of pleasure?

No, the voice says, we cannot.

The author wishes to thank Denise Dembinski for her editorial eye, and Solange Aurora Cheney for her forbearance through the years.

About the Author

Glenn Alan Cheney is a writer, translator, journalist, artist and managing editor of New London Librarium. He has written more than 40 books on such topics as the Pilgrims, cats, Linmcoln, nuns, Swaziland, Brazil's Estrada Real, Brazil's Quilombo dos Palmares, environmental issues in Amazonia, death and burial, bees, and Chernobyl. He has also written novels, essays, poetry and op-ed columns. He lives in Hanover, Conn.

www.ingramcontent.com/pod-product-compliance
Lightning Source LLC
Chambersburg PA
CBHW030544310726
48979CB00010B/2023/J

* 9 7 8 1 9 4 7 0 7 4 8 1 1 *